PUFFIN

ᴅancing

OUT OF STEP

Antonia Barber was born in London and grew up in Sussex. While studying English at London University, she spent her evenings at the Royal Opera House, where her father worked, watching the ballet and meeting many famous dancers. She married a fellow student and lived in New York before settling back in England. She has three children, including a daughter who did ballet from the age of three and attended the Royal Ballet School Junior Classes at Sadler's Wells.

Her best-known books are *The Ghosts*, which was runner-up for the Carnegie Medal and was filmed as *The Amazing Mr Blunden*, and *The Mousehole Cat*. She has also written *Tales from the Ballet*.

Antonia lives in an old oast house in Kent and a little fisherman's cottage in Cornwall.

If you like dancing and making friends, you'll love

DANCING SHOES

Lucy Lambert – Lou to her friends – dreams of one day becoming a great ballerina. Find out if Lucy's dream comes true in:

DANCING SHOES: LESSONS FOR LUCY
DANCING SHOES: INTO THE SPOTLIGHT
DANCING SHOES: FRIENDS AND RIVALS
DANCING SHOES: MAKING THE GRADE
(coming in 1999)

And look out for more DANCING SHOES titles coming soon

Antonia Barber

DANCING SHOES
Out of Step

Illustrated by Biz Hull

PUFFIN BOOKS

PUFFIN BOOKS

Published by the Penguin Group
Penguin Books Ltd, 27 Wrights Lane, London W8 5TZ, England
Penguin Putnam Inc., 375 Hudson Street, New York, New York 10014, USA
Penguin Books Australia Ltd, Ringwood, Victoria, Australia
Penguin Books Canada Ltd, 10 Alcorn Avenue, Toronto, Ontario, Canada M4V 3B2
Penguin Books (NZ) Ltd, Private Bag 102902, NSMC, Auckland, New Zealand

Penguin Books Ltd, Registered Offices: Harmondsworth, Middlesex, England

First published 1998
5 7 9 10 8 6

Text copyright © Antonia Barber, 1998
Illustrations copyright © Biz Hull, 1998
All rights reserved

The moral right of the author and illustrator has been asserted

Made and printed in England by Clays Ltd, St Ives plc

British Library Cataloguing in Publication Data
A CIP catalogue record for this book is available from the British Library

ISBN 0–140–38685–8

Chapter One

Lucy Lambert sat back in her seat and watched the trees and houses flash past as the train sped through the London suburbs. Her mother, Jenny, sat with eyes closed and Charlie asleep on her lap. It was hard to keep awake after the long journey from Cornwall, but Lou knew that they would soon be pulling into Paddington Station, which meant putting on coats and sorting out Charlie's

pushchair and the luggage.

What was Emma doing now? Lucy pictured her looking out of the window, counting the minutes until her best friend's return. The Lamberts lived in the basement of the Brownes' house, which suited both girls very well.

Poor Emma! She had told Lou in her postcard that her granny had come to look after her for the last few days of the half-term holiday, while her parents were abroad. Lou had never actually met Granny Browne, but she knew from Emma that the old lady was very bossy and was always making people do things they didn't want to do. She had made Emma's father work in a bank when he wanted to be a carpenter . . .

That reminded Lou. 'Do you think our new kitchen will be finished?' she asked her mother.

Jenny opened her eyes and smiled. 'Yes, I think so. Mr Browne said he was going to do it at the beginning of the week, before they went to Rome. Won't it be brilliant to be rid of that awful old sink and to have hot water all the time?'

'Great!' said Lou, and then, 'Do you

think Granny Browne will have gone
home by now?'

'No, I think she's staying until
tomorrow. Mr and Mrs Browne are flying
home late tonight.'

'Fancy going to Rome just for a few
days,' said Lou. 'It must cost an awful
lot!'

'Well, maybe when I've passed my
exams and got a better job, we can go
abroad too,' said Jenny. She had begun to
put Charlie's coat on and he was
protesting sleepily.

'I'd rather go to Cornwall,' said Lou.
They had been staying with her
grandparents and Lou's grandma was
very different from Granny Browne. She
loved everyone and never made them do
things they didn't want to. Grandad was

4

brilliant too: he built marvellous sandcastles and made dams and canals all over the beach. And when Charlie jumped on them, he just laughed.

'Better get your coat on,' said Jenny, 'while I lift the bags down.'

In the taxi Lou sat on the little seat that folded down.

'Are you sorry to be back?' asked Jenny, as they headed north.

Lou smiled at her. 'Not really . . . I mean, I can't wait to see Emma . . . but it was lovely staying with Grandma and Grandad.'

'Even though Grandma spent most of her time fussing over Charlie?'

'Well . . .' Lou had felt a bit neglected this time.

'You mustn't mind,' said her mother.

'Remember that when Daddy died, she lost her only son. Charlie is very like him when he was a baby. It brings back happy memories for her.'

'Yes,' said Lou, 'I suppose so . . . She's still got Auntie Helen.'

'But she lives in Canada,' said her mother, 'so they don't see her very often . . . They both loved your dancing,' she added.

That was true, thought Lou. She had danced for them a lot and had told them all about her ballet lessons and about Emma and Jem, who was the only boy in the class. Grandad had said that if boys could do ballet, he wanted to learn. He had made Lou show him all the *pliés* and *tendus*, and how to do a *révérence*. But everyone had laughed so much at his

efforts that he had given up. Still, they
had both promised to come to her first
night when she was a famous ballerina
and danced at the Opera House!

She wondered what Jem had been doing during the holiday, and whether he had seen horrible Angela . . .

But at that moment the taxi pulled up outside the tall terraced house and it was time to unload everything.

Chapter Two

The kitchen looked wonderful. It was
very small, but it now had a shiny clean
sink set in a smooth green worktop.
There was a little white heater which
gave a stream of hot water when you
turned the knob. There were pine
cupboards and tiles on the floor and . . .

'Oh, Lou! We've even got a new
cooker!'

Jenny looked as if she might burst into

tears, which was a bit odd as Lou knew
she was very happy. She hugged her
mother and said, 'Mr Browne is really
kind, isn't he?'

Jenny sniffed hard and said, 'Very
kind.'

'Shall I go up and thank him?' asked
Lou.

'Well, he won't be home yet, but you
could go and see Emma and tell her how
pleased we are.'

Lou had quite forgotten about Emma
in the excitement of the new kitchen.
Now she thought it was strange that Em
had not already come clattering down the
stairs.

'I will,' she said. 'I'll go and tell her
that her dad is great!'

At the top of the basement stairs, the

Brownes' kitchen door stood ajar. Lou rushed straight in, and came face to face with a small, thin woman with blue-grey hair. The woman frowned at her and Lou knew at once that it must be Granny Browne.

'Oh . . . sorry! I was looking for Emma.'

The woman had sharp little eyes and stared at her with her head on one side. Lou felt like a caterpillar being sized up by a hungry bird.

'I . . . I came to say that the new kitchen is lovely,' she stammered.

'The new kitchen?' It was clear that Granny Browne knew nothing about it.

'In our basement,' Lou explained. 'Mr Browne fitted it while we were in Cornwall.'

'Huh! My son has more money than sense,' sniffed the old woman.

Lou thought this was pretty rude.

'Well,' she said, 'I'll just go up to Emma's room, shall I?'

'She's not there,' said Granny Browne. 'She's gone to visit Angela –'

'Angela!' Lou let out a yelp of protest.

'Such a *delightful* girl,' went on the old woman smugly. 'And such a *lovely* house! They get on so well together, and as for her grandfather . . . what a *charming* man!'

Lou felt as if a large black hole had suddenly opened up in her world. She had only been gone for a week and everything had changed. Emma, her *best friend*, had gone to see horrible Angela. And Angela's grandfather, who was really nice, seemed to have made friends with bossy Granny Browne. She wondered bitterly if Jem was also round at Angela's and if she had any friends left!

Then she remembered Mrs Dillon in the top-floor flat. *She* would still be there . . . Or would she?

'Is Mrs Dillon in?' she asked. 'I might go up and see her.'

'I'm sure I've no idea where *she* is,' said Granny Browne. It was clear that she did not like Mrs Dillon.

Oh good, thought Lou; at least I've got one friend left.

She saw that the Brownes' table was set for tea with four plates and some delicious cream cakes. Emma must be coming back for tea, and bringing Angela and her grandfather with her. The kitchen clock showed almost tea-time and Lou didn't want to be there when they arrived.

'I'll be off then,' she said.

Granny Browne seemed pleased to get rid of her.

Lou climbed to the top of the house, and here at least she found an ally. Mrs Dillon had once been a Russian ballet dancer

and had given Lou her first dancing
lessons. She welcomed her into the cosy
attic, making hot chocolate and getting
out some Viennese biscuits.

Lou poured out her tale of woe.

'Pouff!' said Mrs Dillon in disgust.
'That Granny Browne! I see the game she
is playing. She is setting her cap at that
nice Mr Mumford.'

It took Lou a minute to
work out who Mr Mumford

was. She always thought of him as 'Angela's grandfather' or 'the Wind-Up Merchant' because he was a terrible tease. And as for 'setting her cap' at him . . .

'What do you mean?' she asked, biting into one of the rich, crumbly biscuits.

'Setting her cap?' said Mrs Dillon. 'It means that she plans to marry him.'

'Marry him?' Lou was astonished. 'But they are both old!'

Mrs Dillon narrowed her eyes and raised her eyebrows. 'You think old people are not allowed to marry?'

'Well, yes . . . of course they are,' said Lou, 'but, I mean, they don't fall in love, do they?'

'It is not unknown,' said Mrs Dillon drily, 'but for *that woman* I think we need not talk of love. He is very rich man; she will marry him for his money!' She lowered her voice and went on, 'Ever since they are meeting up in the market, she is asking him to tea and making him take them all to the ballet.'

'To the ballet!' Lou couldn't believe it. 'Emma went to the ballet? . . . With Angela? . . . And the Wind-Up Merchant? . . . While I was *away*?'

Mrs Dillon nodded.

Lou felt like crying. She took a few comforting mouthfuls of the hot chocolate and then said, 'Well, at least Granny Browne is going home tomorrow.'

Mrs Dillon sniffed. 'Pouff!' she said. '*She'll be back!*'

Chapter Three

On her way back to the basement, Lou passed the Brownes' kitchen door. It was still slightly open and Granny Browne's voice rose above the sound of clinking teacups.

'My son is refitting the basement flat for me,' she was saying, 'so that I can move in as soon as the Lamberts have gone.'

Lou stopped dead. She knew she

shouldn't eavesdrop, but this was serious! Perhaps Mr Browne wasn't being kind; perhaps he was planning to get rid of them! But she remembered that Granny Browne had not known about the new kitchen . . .

Then she heard Emma's voice. 'Lou isn't moving out! You know she's not!'

'Not at once, of course,' said Granny

Browne in a sickly-sweet voice. 'But when Mrs Lambert passes her exams and gets a better job, she is sure to want a bigger flat. And then you will be able to run downstairs and see Granny whenever you like. Won't that be nice?'

'I don't want them to go,' said Emma. She sounded really upset. 'Oh, I wish Lou was back.'

Granny Browne didn't tell her that Lou *was* back and Lou couldn't just burst in . . . not with Angela there. But she went downstairs feeling much better.

Even if Emma had been to the ballet with Angela, it was clear that Lou was still her best friend.

It was not until Emma was seeing her visitors out that she noticed the light in the basement. She was down the stairs in a flash, hugging Lou and Jenny and swinging Charlie around.

'Oh, I'm so glad you're all back!' she

said, flushed and breathless. 'I did miss you so much.'

'What have you been doing?' asked Lou, as if she didn't know.

'Oh, well . . .' Emma turned pink and looked very guilty (and so you should, thought Lou unkindly).

Emma brightened. 'Well,' she said, 'the first half of the week I helped Dad to do your kitchen. Do you like it?'

'It's amazing!' said Lou. 'And your dad is great!'

'I did some of the painting,' said Emma proudly, 'with a roller thing. It was fun!'

'And the second half of the week?' asked Lou.

'Oh, that . . .' Emma went pink again. 'Well,' she began slowly, and then it all came out in a rush. 'Mum and Dad went to Rome and Granny Browne came and we met the Wind-Up Merchant in the market . . . with Angela . . . and Granny Browne asked them to tea and then Angela's grandfather asked us to tea at *his* house and . . .'

'Did you go anywhere *interesting*?' asked Lou, trying to make her get to the point.

'Well, Granny Browne said she would take me to see a ballet and invited Angela to come too. And then she kept telling Mr Mumford that she didn't know how we could get to the theatre because it was somewhere in south London. So he had to offer to take us in his car, and in the end he bought the tickets and everything . . .' Her voice trailed away.

Lou left her to suffer in silence for a while and then said, 'And was it good?'

'Oh, yes,' said Emma eagerly. 'Well, it wasn't as good as at the Opera House . . .' she backtracked hastily. 'But it was fun.'

'Which ballet was it?' asked Lou. If it was *Romeo and Juliet*, she thought, I shall die!

But Emma said, 'It had a French name, something about "magic". It was about a little boy who lost his temper and then all the things in his room came to life: the books, the teapot, even the wallpaper . . .'

'It sounds like *L'Enfant et les Sortilèges*,' put in Jenny, who was getting Charlie into his sleepsuit. 'It means *The Boy and the Magic*.'

'That's it!' said Emma.

Lou thought it sounded quite good.

She was really cross that she had missed it, but it did seem as though it wasn't Emma's fault. 'Poor old you,' she said, 'having to go with Angela.'

'Well . . . she's all right really,' said Emma slowly. 'When you get to know her, I mean. She said she wanted to be my best friend, but I said *you* were my *best* friend. And she is going to be really nice to me at school,' she added hopefully.

'Huh!' Lou's voice was scornful, but Jenny said quickly, 'Well, that's good news, isn't it, Lou? I mean, we do want Emma to be happy at school, don't we?'

She said it in a special sort of voice and Lou found that she had to agree.

Chapter Four

As they hurried up the front steps of the
Maple School of Ballet on Wednesday,
it was Lou who was now the anxious
one. For two whole terms Angela had
bullied Emma. Now suddenly they were
friends. So what was Angela up to? she
wondered. And who was going to be her
next victim?

She soon found out.

As they entered the crowded changing

room, Angela and her cronies clustered around Emma, welcoming her as if she was their best friend. They didn't even look at Lou. They seemed to be making a wall between her and Emma as they pulled on their tights and stretched into their pale-blue leotards.

Oh, it's like that, is it? thought Lou. See if I care! You can't bully me. I don't even go to your stupid private school! And she smiled and chatted to the younger ones, who greeted her with their usual friendliness.

Emma seemed embarrassed. She pushed her way through the older girls and began to do Lou's hair. She and Lou always took turns to do each other's hair, smoothing it back and twisting it into a neat bun under a little blue bun-net. But

27

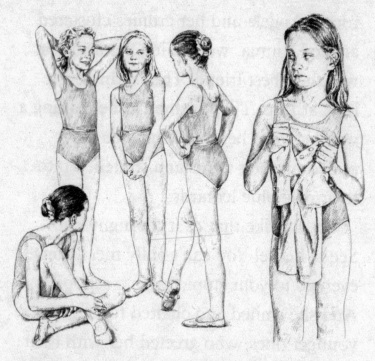

now, as Lou stood waiting patiently for
Emma to finish, Angela came up behind
them and began to do Emma's hair for
her. And *Emma didn't stop her*!

Lou felt outraged. Angela was acting as
if she *owned* Emma. As soon as her own
hair was fixed, she growled her 'Thanks'

and flounced out of the changing room. As she passed, Angela glanced up with her sly, cat-like smile. It said, as clearly as if she had spoken, 'Emma is *my* friend now.'

In the studio, Jem was waiting.

'Oh-oh!' he said when he saw Lou's face. 'What has Angela done now?'

Lou told him.

'So?' he said annoyingly. 'I thought we wanted Angela to be nice to her. Remember how miserable Em was last term.'

'Well . . . yes,' said Lou, 'but now *I'm* being left out.'

'Oh, come on, Lou,' said Jem. 'You've got loads of friends at our school. And Emma needs to be friends with Angela and the others at her school.'

'Yes . . . but Angela's doing it on purpose . . . to get at me,' said Lou.

Boys don't understand, she thought. Emma's my *best* friend. What if she starts to like Angela more than me?

'It's not as if you're shy, like Emma,' Jem went on. 'You're as tough as an old boot.' He said it admiringly, but Lou was not pleased. An old boot! she thought crossly.

But before she could protest, the others came in, followed by Mrs Dennison calling, 'Do hurry up and find your places.'

The girls did their *révérences*, Jem did his elegant bow and the class began.

Lou tried to concentrate on her dancing. *Demi-plié, plié, tendu, glissé . . .* every step must be just right. *Arm positions, head position* . . . she would show that she could match Angela every step of the way . . . even if the blonde girl had been taking ballet lessons for much longer. She worked really hard and glowed with pride when Mrs Dennison said, 'Well done, Lucy.'

But she wasn't doing quite so well with her *pas de chat* – the cat-leap. This was a little sideways spring from turned-out, bent knees and Lou's knees never felt quite right. Angela did it perfectly, leaping sideways as effortlessly as the cat she was.

I must practise it, thought Lou. I'll do it again and again and again until I get it just right.

Mrs Dennison had reminded them that the Maple School held its Annual Display and Competition at the end of the Easter term. The parents came to watch and prizes were awarded to the best dancers. Angela had won the class prize for the last two years and Lou reckoned it was time someone else had it. And that someone, she thought, is going to be me.

When the class was over, it was just as bad in the changing room. Angela and her friends crowded around Emma, and Lou made no attempt to break through. They were still surrounding her when they all poured out on to the steps, where Angela's mother was waiting in her big car. The girls piled in.

'Come on, Emma,' called Angela. 'There's room for you.'

Emma hesitated; she looked hopefully at Lou. But Lou wouldn't look at her as

she and Jem walked down the steps.
Emma glanced at Angela, who smiled
sweetly, and then back at Lou and Jem.

Then Jem settled it by saying, 'Come
on, Emma, don't leave me alone with
Miss Grumpy here.'

Gratefully, Emma waved to Angela and turned to join her old friends. Lou tried to stay cross, but Jem started clowning about until she had to laugh. The three of them walked home together, and before long it was like old times.

Chapter Five

Mrs Dillon had been right about Granny
Browne. Only a week had gone by and
already *she was back*.

'She says her boiler isn't working
properly,' Emma told Lou. 'She made
Daddy drive all the way down to
Worthing to fetch her. And now she's
here, she keeps on about how much
better it would be if she lived in your
basement.'

'We are not moving!' said Lou fiercely.

'Or Mrs Dillon's attic,' added Emma in a wail.

'Don't worry,' said Lou. 'Mrs Dillon would never move out to please your granny. She can't stand her.'

'Granny Browne is just as bad,' said Emma. 'She's always saying unkind things about Mrs Dillon. She says she doesn't believe she was a Bolshoi dancer . . . that she's old and her mind is wandering.'

'I expect she's jealous,' said Lou wisely.

'I thought it was just children who were horrible to each other,' said Emma. 'I thought grown-ups sort of . . . grew out of it.'

'They do all sorts of things you wouldn't expect,' Lou told her. 'I mean

. . . I didn't know old people got married.'

'Do they?' said Emma. 'I wish someone would marry Granny Browne.'

'Mrs Dillon says she's planning to marry the Wind-Up Merchant.'

Emma stared at Lou in horror. 'But that's dreadful!' she said. 'I mean . . . the Wind-Up Merchant is really nice. It wouldn't be fair to him . . . or us, because she'd live much too close. Why can't she marry someone in Worthing?'

'Or Scotland?' suggested Lou, grinning.

'Or Rome?' Emma giggled.

'The moon?'

'Mars?'

They fell about at the thought of Granny Browne married to a Little Green Man.

*

On Jenny Lambert's evening-class night,
Mrs Dillon always came down to baby-sit
for Charlie. At the same time, she held a
practice ballet class for Lou, Emma and
Jem. Mr Browne had fixed up a big old
mirror and a *barre* in Emma's room. But
this week she had gone to a birthday
party for one of the girls at her school
(Lou tried hard not to mind).

Mrs Dillon said they would practise in
Lou's living room; she would not use
Emma's room if she wasn't there. 'I am
not having some old woman make snidey
remarks to me!' she said with her nose in
the air.

It was a nuisance because they could
not see their mistakes and had to hold on
to chair-backs, which were never quite the

right height. (*First position, right hand on chair, left hand on waist . . . into second, heels down, head up . . . and down into* demi-plié.) Lou dipped and rose with a wonderful feeling that the movement now came naturally to her. (*Turn about, left hand on chair . . . and start again.*) It was like Charlie learning to walk, all awkward and wobbly at first . . . (*Bend knees . . . smoothly and gracefully, up.*) But if you did it often enough, your brain got sort of programmed . . . like the computers at school (*and close into first position*) . . . and then you only had to think *plié* or *tendu* or *glissé* and it came out just right! Except for the *pas de chat* . . . I need to practise it every day, she thought. Real dancers practise every day even when they are good enough to dance on stage.

But Mrs Dillon got quite cross with her pupils if they practised alone. 'One hour with your teacher, doing steps correctly,' she would say, 'and then what you do? You go home and practise alone and you are doing it just a little bit wrong . . . and next time a little bit more wrong. And maybe you are twisting your ankles a little and they grow weak instead of strong. No! Real dancers

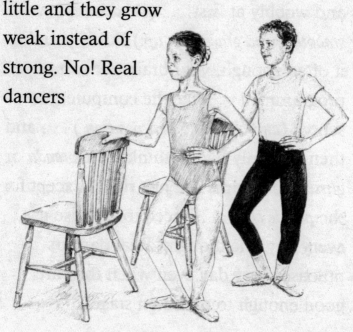

practise each day, it is true. But always the teacher is with them and watches with the eye of an eagle!'

Lou knew that she was right. But she did so want to practise her *pas de chat*.

After the class they sat and talked.

'I have news!' said Mrs Dillon. 'It is Irina Barashkova who will judge your end-of-term competition.'

'Really? Oh, great!' said Jem. He knew that this had been Mrs Dillon's name when she was a young dancer with the Bolshoi.

'T'rific!' said Lou. 'That means we'll win all the prizes. I mean, we must be the best, stands to reason, because you are our teacher!'

She was teasing, but Mrs Dillon frowned. 'There is being no favouritism,' she said very sternly. 'Indeed, I shall be more hard on you, young lady, than on the others. When you are making little, tiny mistake, I think, "How many times I tell that girl not to do that thing!" And so I give you *very* bad marks!'

Lou stared at her in dismay. It was not until she noticed the grin on Jem's face that she realized Mrs Dillon could also tease.

Chapter Six

Jenny Lambert finished her chat with the stallholder, gathered up her fruit and vegetables, and moved on.

Lou trailed behind with the pushchair. There was a fine rain falling and the street market seemed dull and boring without her friends. Jem had gone to a football match with his grandad and Emma was shopping for new shoes with Granny Browne. She had wanted to take

Lou with her to help her choose, but
Granny Browne had made it very clear
that Lou was not welcome.

She wants to split us up, thought Lou
gloomily. She wants Angela to be
Emma's friend instead of me. Was it just
because Angela was richer and
Granny Browne liked rich
people? Or was it part of her
cunning plan to marry
Angela's
grandfather?

Old people

should know better than to go around marrying other old people, she thought crossly. If Granny Browne married the Wind-Up Merchant, then Emma and Angela would have the same grandparents! They would start spending Christmas together . . . and going on holidays together . . . They would go to the ballet a lot and Granny Browne (only she would be Granny Mumford then) would *never* invite Lou. She pictured Emma and Angela, in ribbons and jewels, sitting side by side in a red and gold box at the ballet, and herself, standing outside the theatre door . . . in the rain.

'Cheer up, Lucy! It may never happen!' It was the Wind-Up Merchant.

Lou jumped a mile, certain that he had been reading her thoughts. She glanced nervously about for Angela, but he seemed to be alone.

Her mother turned to greet him and he said, 'Your Lou seems down in the dumps, Mrs Lambert. May I cheer her up with a cream cake and some lemonade? I still owe her for helping me with my magic show at Angela's birthday party.'

'I'm sure she'd love it,' said Jenny.

Lou had an odd feeling that her mum had known Mr Mumford would turn up . . . that they were up to something. Still, she was thirsty and the Wind-Up Merchant was leading the way towards the Cosy Corner, the best cake shop in town.

Five minutes later, with her mouth full of meringue and a big blob of cream on the end of her nose, she was feeling much better. They were chatting about the magic show and the Wind-Up Merchant was really pleased when Lou told him that she had not given away the magic secrets.

'Lucy Lambert, you are a real professional!' he said admiringly, and Lou glowed.

There was a brief silence while she wrestled with the meringue, which was very large and seemed to explode when you bit into it.

Then he said, 'I'm sorry you missed the ballet. I would have invited you, but you were away.'

Lou smiled at him and discovered the blob of cream on the end of her nose. While she was dealing with it, he went on, 'It's a touring company and they are doing *La Fille Mal Gardée* next week.'

Lou knew all about this ballet. It was in Emma's *Tales from the Ballet* book, where it was called *The Girl Who Needed Watching*. It was very funny . . . but why was he telling her about it?

As she swallowed her mouthful of meringue, he said, 'I thought we might all go together, you and me and Emma . . . and Angela.'

For a moment Lou's heart leapt. Then she shook her head. 'Angela won't want me to come,' she said.

'*I* want you to come,' said the Wind-Up Merchant.

'But she'll be horrible to me,' said Lou gloomily.

There was a silence, and then he said, 'You don't like Angela, do you?'

Lou didn't know what to say.

'May I ask you why?' he said gently.

Lou hesitated, not wanting to say mean things about his granddaughter.

'Be honest,' he said. 'I need to know.'

'Well,' said Lou at last, 'she bullies people. She was really awful to Emma last term. She made all the other girls ignore her.'

'Yes . . . I know.' He looked very sad

and Lou felt dreadful. 'But they are friends now,' he said hopefully. 'Couldn't you be her friend too?'

But Lou felt sure that Angela was only being nice to Emma to get back at her. She said nothing and he went on, 'She needs a friend like you, Lucy . . . someone who would stand up to her . . . someone she couldn't push around.'

But Lou knew that Angela hated anyone she couldn't push around.

'Will you give it a try?' said the Wind-Up Merchant. 'Will you come to the ballet with us? It will be my thank-you for helping me with the magic show.'

Lou had a sudden thought. 'Will Granny Browne be going?' she asked.

He smiled. 'Oh yes. I think I should take Emma's grandmother to help me keep you all in order! There's another friend Angela wants to invite too . . . one of the boys from her ballet class.'

There *was* only one boy in the ballet class . . . and that was Jem. So Angela was trying to take both Lou's friends away!

But for the moment that seemed less important than the fact that the Wind-Up Merchant had smiled when she mentioned Granny Browne. Lou felt that she had to warn him . . . She plucked up all her courage.

'Mrs Dillon says she is setting her cap at you,' she blurted out. 'Granny Browne, I mean . . . And I know you wouldn't be happy if you married her . . . She would just make you do things you didn't want to do, all the time!'

When she had said it, she turned bright pink. The Wind-Up Merchant was staring at her in astonishment. Lou felt like dying.

Then slowly his face changed and he grew very solemn. 'You think it would be a mistake?' he asked.

'Yes,' said Lou earnestly. 'Yes, I do.'

'Hmmm.' He thought for a while, then he said, 'Suppose we make a bargain, you and I. You come to the ballet and try to be friends with Angela . . . and I'll promise not to marry Granny Browne.'

Lou could have hugged him. It was such a relief. 'It's a deal!' she said.

He held out his hand, palm up, and she slapped it to seal the bargain. She was just thinking how pleased Emma would be when he lowered his voice and added,

'But you must never tell anyone – not one of your friends, I mean – in case Granny Browne finds out.'

Oh, rats! thought Lou. She really wanted to tell someone.

'Except your mother,' he added. 'A girl should never have secrets from her mother.'

Lou cheered up. She felt sure her mother would be pleased. And it was better if no one else knew. Because if Granny Browne ever found out what she had done . . . Lou shuddered.

'All right,' she promised. 'I won't tell any of my friends . . . only my mum.'

'And I know how well you can keep a secret,' said the Wind-Up Merchant.

It was true, thought Lou, she had kept the secrets of the magic tricks . . . even

from Jem. She smiled at the Wind-Up
Merchant, feeling very pleased that she
had saved him from Granny Browne.

He smiled back. 'And now I shall buy
you another meringue,' he said. 'I do so
like watching you eat them.'

But Lou was full up. 'Um . . . could
I, please, take it with me . . . in a bag?'
she asked. 'You see, my mum loves
meringues, and so does Charlie.'

He bought her a whole boxful.

Chapter Seven

Emma came down to the basement
kitchen carrying a pair of really horrible
shoes. She looked as if she might burst
into tears. 'Look!' she said. 'Aren't they
awful? I just hate them!'

Lou tried to think of something nice to
say about the shoes, but couldn't. 'Why
did you buy them?' she asked.

'Why do you think?' said Emma
miserably. '*She* made me have them.'

'Granny Browne?' asked Lou.

'Yes, Granny Browne!'

Lou's mum came to look. 'Oh dear,' she said. 'I see what you mean.'

They all stood staring at the offending shoes.

'Maybe you could change them,' suggested Lou.

'She'd never let me,' said Emma. 'You don't know her.'

'Have a word with your mum,' advised Jenny. 'Choose a moment when your granny isn't around. Tell her that you really hate the shoes. She'll understand.'

'Do you think so?' Emma looked hopeful.

'Trust me,' said Jenny, 'and trust your mum too.'

The girls took themselves off into Lou's room. Lou couldn't wait to tell Emma about her meeting with the Wind-Up Merchant . . . and about the trip to the ballet.

'It's *The Girl Who Needed Watching*,' she explained, 'only it's got some French name. It's one of those in your *Tales from the Ballet* book. And he's invited me and he's going to invite you and Jem, so there will be three of us and we can deal with Angela between us!'

'You won't quarrel with her?' said Emma anxiously. 'I mean, you can't, not if he's invited us.'

'I'm not going to quarrel with her,' said Lou patiently. 'In fact,' she added, 'I've promised to be nice to her.'

Emma still looked worried. Lou wished she could tell her why she had promised and how she had put a stop to Granny Browne's cunning plan. But it was a secret and wild horses wouldn't drag it from her. She sighed.

'I only meant,' she said, 'that if there are three of *us* and only one of *her*, Angela can't leave one of us out.'

'Will Granny Browne be there?' asked Emma.

''Fraid so!' said Lou. 'But Mr Mumford didn't talk about her as if he wanted to marry her.' It was as close as she could get to telling Emma that the danger had passed.

Emma was not convinced.

'Huh!' she said. 'It's not what *he* wants that matters. I mean, *I* didn't want to buy the shoes!'

For a moment, Lou also had doubts. But the Wind-Up Merchant had promised.

'Trust me!' she told Emma in the sort of confident voice her mother had used. 'It will be all right.'

Emma took the horrible shoes back upstairs and brought down *Tales from the*

Ballet. They sat side by side on Lou's bed and read *The Girl Who Needed Watching*. It was about a girl whose mother was trying to make her marry a man she didn't love because he was rich. The mother reminded them both of Granny Browne. Luckily the girl wasn't just pretty, she was clever too. She got the better of her bossy mother and married the poor but honest young man she really loved. They both agreed that if they had to go to the ballet with Granny Browne, this would be a good one to watch.

On practice night they had some good news.

'That nice Mr Mumford is inviting me to the ballet,' announced Mrs Dillon. 'He tells me that you three will be coming too.'

'And Angela,' said Lou.

'And Granny Browne,' sighed Emma.

'Life is never perfect,' said Mrs Dillon. 'But we shall be having very good time.'

Lou tried hard to keep her mind on her practice . . . especially her *pas de chat*. But she kept imagining Mrs Dillon and

Granny Browne at the ballet together. Did the Wind-Up Merchant have any idea what he was taking on? She had a sudden picture of the two old ladies coming to blows – she saw them both armed with umbrellas . . .

'This *pas de chat* you are doing is more like a *pas de grenouille*,' said Mrs Dillon crossly. 'Please to keep your mind on your dancing, Lucy!'

'What's a *gronwee*?' asked Lou.

'It is a – how are you saying it? – a frog!' said Mrs Dillon.

Lou was horrified. A *pas de frog*? How awful! I must practise more, I must get it right! she thought. I've just got to beat Angela!

Chapter Eight

There were seven of them going to the ballet, so they needed two cars. Mr Browne took Emma, Lou, Granny Browne and Mrs Dillon, leaving Angela and her grandfather to pick up Jem. Lou and Emma wished they could swap Jem for Granny Browne so they could all be together.

Travelling south to the theatre, they were both very excited. They sat in the back with Mrs Dillon who told them the history of the ballet. She said that *La Fille Mal Gardée* was very special as it was the first ever ballet about ordinary people.

'Before this, ballet was being mostly about gods and goddesses,' she told them, 'but this is tale of simple peasants.'

'So was *Giselle*,' Lou reminded her.

'This is true, but *Giselle* is being written much later. Also this ballet is telling a real story and making people laugh, which was not done in ballet before.'

'I like the bit in the story where Lise tricks her mother into letting her marry Colas,' said Lou.

'The mother is *awful*,' said Emma. 'She is always trying to make her daughter do things she doesn't want to do.' She spoke with great feeling and Lou heard an angry snort from Granny Browne in the front seat. The old lady was sulking. She hated it when Mrs Dillon was the centre of attention.

They arrived first and were all waiting on the pavement when the other car pulled up. Jem jumped out of the front seat and opened the back door of the car with a flourish. Angela tossed her long blonde hair and emerged, long legs first, trying to look like a supermodel. She smiled briefly at Emma, ignored Lou, and glued herself to Jem's side.

The theatre was very modern, not at all like the grand, old-fashioned Opera House. Their seats were near the front of the balcony and Angela led the way along the row.

Jem was following close behind her but

he stepped aside suddenly. 'Ladies first,'
he said, and waved Emma and Lou
ahead of him. Lou wondered if he was
just being polite or whether he had done
it on purpose so that he could sit next to
her instead of Angela.

The bad news was that he now had

Granny Browne sitting on the other side of him . . . But not for long. Granny Browne had pushed ahead, like Angela, but when she saw that the Wind-Up Merchant was sitting next to Mrs Dillon, she stood up again.

'Oh dear,' she said, 'I seem to have left my handkerchief in my coat pocket,' and she squeezed out along the row. But when she came back, instead of returning to her own seat, she said to Angela's grandfather, 'It will be easier if you move along.'

So Mrs Dillon moved next to Jem and Granny Browne settled herself triumphantly beside her prey.

Lou and Emma had a fit of the giggles.

'She did that on purpose,' whispered Emma.

'I bet her hanky was in her pocket all
the time,' hissed Lou.

Angela glared at them both. Lou
decided that she was probably wishing
she had thought of the same trick to sit
next to Jem. But then she remembered
her promise and was just returning
Angela's glare with her sweetest smile
when the lights went down.

The ballet was wonderful. It was lively

and full of colour and very funny. There
was a graceful dance with ribbons and a
comic dance by some big chickens which
made them all laugh. Alain, the rich
farmer's son, danced with his umbrella,
and the bossy mother, who was played by
a man like a pantomime dame, danced in
wooden clogs. Even the romantic scenes
were funny, with Colas stealing kisses
from Lise whenever Alain's back was
turned. The bit Lou liked best was when
Lise, thinking she was alone, dreamed of
her wedding day. She did not know that
Colas was watching her and was very
embarrassed when he appeared, but it all
ended happily.

Travelling home, Lou and Emma
agreed that it had been one of the best
evenings in their whole lives!

'It was much better than going with Angela when you were away,' whispered Emma, but Granny Browne's sharp ears heard her.

'I think, Emma, that we may look forward to many more ballet trips with dear Angela,' she said smugly. 'Mr Mumford is so charming and *so* attentive.'

In your dreams, thought Lou, and wondered what Granny Browne would say if she knew about the Wind-Up Merchant's promise. But then she remembered that she had also promised . . . to try to be friends with Angela . . . and she hadn't tried very hard. Would the Wind-Up Merchant keep *his* promise if she didn't keep *hers*? It was a worrying thought.

Chapter Nine

It was the final lesson before the Maple School's Annual Display and Competition. Lou tried hard to keep her mind on her dancing. She was standing behind Angela and it depressed her to see how well her rival danced. She comforted herself with the knowledge that after two terms of lessons, she was pretty good herself. Mrs Dillon's coaching had made all the difference. She was so strict: she would never let Lou get away with even the smallest ugly movement.

Oh, if only I could beat Angela, she thought. In her mind's eye she saw Angela's face, white and furious, as she heard the applause and saw Lou walking forward to take the cup . . . Her mind was wandering again! Mrs Dillon said it was her worst fault. But Lou's head was always buzzing with thoughts and pictures. It was like having a brightly coloured video screen inside her head . . . She reached firmly for the 'off' switch.

At their last practice session she asked Mrs Dillon if she could concentrate on her *pas de chat*. She had not forgotten the old lady's remark about the *pas de frog*. Sometimes she got it just right, but at

other times it was as if she tried too hard. Her muscles grew tense and at once she lost that fluid, cat-like grace.

On the night before the Display she could not sleep. She was worried and over-

excited and, to make things worse,
Charlie was being fretful because he had
lost his teddy bear. Jenny finally
persuaded him to take his woolly
elephant to bed instead and he dozed off
muttering and complaining.

Lou lay in the dark and worried about
being awake.

Jenny heard her tossing and turning.
'Can't you sleep?' she asked softly,
appearing in the doorway.

'No,' said Lou miserably, 'and if I don't
I'll be all tired tomorrow and my dancing
will be awful.'

'Is something worrying you?'

'Well . . . there's this thing called a *pas
de chat*. Sometimes I get it right and
sometimes I don't.'

'You'll get it right tomorrow,' said her

mother. 'Try not to worry about it.'

'I can't help it,' said Lou, 'and now I'm worrying about worrying.'

'You need some milk and honey,' said Jenny. 'That will soon make you sleepy.'

Lou accepted gratefully and, comforted by the rich, warm drink, drifted off into a restless sleep.

She woke in the night. The house was silent and her room in darkness. Switching on her little bedside lamp, she saw that her alarm clock showed half-past three. She needed to go to the loo: it was either nerves or that hot drink, she thought crossly. She made her way to the bathroom, moving quietly so as not to wake her mother or Charlie.

Sitting on the loo, she thought about

the ballet competition. If only she got the *pas de chat* right, she was in with a chance. If I was really being friendly to Angela, she thought, I wouldn't be so desperate to beat her . . . But Angela had won it for the last two years and maybe that had helped to make her so snooty and superior. The Wind-Up Merchant said she needed someone to stand up to her. Perhaps Lou beating her in the competition was just what he wanted.

As she made her way back to her bedroom, she thought about the *pas de chat*. It was just a matter of relaxing, of making her muscles loose and easy so that the movement flowed . . . It wouldn't hurt to practise it a few times, then she could stop worrying about it. She could see well enough by the bedside lamp and

her bare feet on the carpet would make
no sound.

Left to right . . . That was it! She had got
it just right! For a moment her whole
body was filled with a sense of the
smoothness and grace of dance perfectly
performed. She suddenly understood how
marvellous it would feel to be a trained
dancer.

Now *right to left* . . . She moved as if in
a dream . . . and suddenly found
Charlie's lost teddy bear. It was jammed
under her bed with one leg sticking out.
In the dim light, Lou's foot caught
against it, throwing her off balance. She
fell headlong, twisting her ankle sideways
as she hit the floor.

She lay on the carpet, holding her
breath, hoping the dull thud would not

wake the others. Slowly the silence settled
about her. Sitting up, she moved the ankle
nervously to see if it hurt. It was a bit
sore, but nothing serious. She decided
that practising in the dim light was not,
after all, a brilliant idea. Climbing into
bed, she turned out the lamp and went
back to sleep.

Chapter Ten

Waking on the morning of the Big Day, Lucy's first thought was for her ankle. *Please, please*, she said to God, *I know I was stupid, but please let my ankle be all right and I promise I'll be good for ever!*

She swung her legs over the side of the bed and cautiously circled her foot. It felt all right. *Oh, thank you! Thank you, God!* (A life of endless goodness loomed ahead of her.) She leapt joyfully off the bed . . .

79

then cried out in pain as her left knee gave way beneath her.

Lou burst into tears. How could God be so mean and sneaky? It was true that she had only bargained for the ankle, but He must have known that she meant the knee as well!

Charlie came in, troubled by the sound of her crying.

'It's all your fault!' she yelled at him. 'You and your stupid teddy bear!'

'Teddy! Teddy!' said Charlie joyfully, catching sight of the leg under the bed. He hauled out the beloved bear and hugged it.

Jenny came in to see what all the shouting was about.

'It's all his fault,' sobbed Lou. 'I tripped over his stupid bear when I went to the

loo in the night . . . and now I've hurt my
knee . . . and I won't be able to dance
properly . . . and Angela will win . . . and
I hate *everyone*!'

Her mother sat on the bed and put her
arms around her. She rocked her in
silence until the worst of the storm had
passed. Then she
said, 'Let's have a

look at the knee.' It didn't even look swollen, but when Lou put her weight upon it, it just seemed to give way. She burst into tears all over again.

'Teddy love Lou,' said Charlie, climbing up beside her.

Lou felt like throwing Teddy out of the window, but she knew she was being unfair. It was her own fault for trying to do the *pas de chat* in the half-light. She gritted her teeth while Charlie made Teddy kiss her better.

The news spread. Emma nearly cried too when she saw Lou's flushed and tear-stained face.

Mrs Dillon examined the knee with an expert eye. 'Is common injury in dancers,' she said. 'A few days will put it right.'

'But the competition is today,' said Lou desperately.

'Ah! Of that there is no question. To dance might do great harm.'

'But I must!' wailed Lou. 'I have to beat Angela!'

'Pouff!' said Mrs Dillon. 'With that knee? You just make big fool of yourself.'

It was true . . . and Lou knew it . . . and there was nothing in the world that she could do about it.

The competition was held in a nearby hall. Lou limped in on her mother's arm with the rest of the audience. Everyone was very kind to her.

Jem's grandmother, Orly Sinclair, kissed her and said, 'Oh, the hazards of a performer's life! For us singers it is the sore throat, for you dancers, the sprained ankle!'

'Actually, it's my knee,' said Lou.

'Knee or ankle, it's a tragedy,' said the Wind-Up Merchant, and he really seemed to mean it. Lou had the feeling again that he had hoped to see his granddaughter take second place for once.

I've let everyone down, she thought miserably.

The little ones performed first and got a lot of applause as they did their final *révérences*. Mrs Dillon, sitting to one side, made notes on the paper in front of her.

Then Lou's class took their places. She hadn't expected to feel quite so left out and upset as she did when she saw them. A tear ran down her cheek and she was glad it was dark. Jenny squeezed her hand and passed her a handkerchief.

As they began the familiar class work, Lou's eyes never moved from Angela. She watched hopefully for a badly placed foot or an awkward arm movement, but she saw none. And yet there was no real pleasure in watching her, thought Lou. Angela's dancing might be perfect, but there was something dull and lifeless about it . . . Not like Jem, who seemed full of bounce and energy. He was pretty good, she had to admit, but she was too busy watching Angela to pay him much attention. And when they reached the end of their performance, she realized with a pang that she had hardly even looked at Emma.

The older classes that followed had

dancers Lou had never seen before, because they went to the ballet school on different nights. It was very exciting to watch the dance steps that she would also do one day.

When they had all finished, there was an interval while Mrs Dillon and Miss Maple put their heads together over the judging. Lou met the Wind-Up Merchant.

'Angela danced really well,' she told him politely.

'She was enchanting,' cooed Granny Browne, who seemed to be following him around.

'Thank you,' he said, but he didn't seem thrilled. 'Now, here is the lady who should be congratulated,' he added, stopping Orly Sinclair as she glided by.

'Your grandson is very impressive,' he told her. 'He has the flair of a natural performer.'

Orly gave him her slow, brilliant smile. 'Your granddaughter also is very talented,' she said.

The two of them stood talking and laughing together while Granny Browne looked on. Her sickly smile faded and her usual cross face returned. Watching her, Lou had a feeling that the old lady knew she would never catch the Wind-Up Merchant now.

'Oh, there you are, Lou.' It was her mother. 'We'd better get back to our seats.'

The prize-giving began. The younger ones came first and a little girl with copper curls proudly carried off her tiny silver cup. Now it was the second class. Lou closed her eyes: she didn't want to see the next bit. She wished she could put her fingers in her ears.

'. . . a dancer whose work is not only correct and well performed,' Mrs Dillon was saying, 'but who also has the spirit and flair of a true dancer . . .'

Spirit and flair? thought Lou. Angela? She must be joking!

And then Mrs Dillon said, 'Jerome Sinclair.'

Lou's eyes flew open, and her mouth too, in a yelp of joy that rang out above the applause. She clapped until her hands hurt. How stupid of her not to have realized that it might be Jem! She had been so carried away by her own battle with Angela, she had not stopped to

think that he might be better than either
of them. She wished now that she had
taken the chance to watch him. In class
he was always at the back, where the girls
couldn't see him.

Lou fretted through the rest of the
presentations. She couldn't wait to
celebrate with Jem and Emma. At last,
the top-class cup had been awarded and it
was all over . . .

Only not quite, it seemed.

Miss Maple was talking to the
audience. '. . . One more cup,' she was
saying, 'and one that often gives us a
problem. But not this year! It goes to a
late starter who has worked very hard
and made exceptional progress.
Unfortunately, a minor accident has

made it impossible for you to see the high standard that she has achieved in only two terms at this school. But we have no hesitation in awarding the Maple Cup for Progress to . . . Lucy Lambert.'

Lou gasped and put her hand to her mouth. She couldn't believe what was happening. Jenny was hauling her to her feet. 'Come on, Lou,' she was saying. 'I'll help you down.'

The applause seemed deafening.

Lou limped through the audience and Miss Maple and Mrs Dillon came down from the stage to meet her. They both kissed her and put the cup (it seemed much bigger than the class cups) into her hands.

Lou turned to face the audience, blinking as the local newspaper's photographer triggered his flash gun. For one glorious moment she was Margot Fonteyn and Darcey Bussell all rolled into one, facing the cheering crowds in a packed theatre. Then the moment passed and she was Lou Lambert again, being hugged and congratulated by her mum and Emma and all her friends . . . and that was even better.

Dancing Shoes

Hi!

I can hardly believe it – being awarded the Maple Cup for Progress was so exciting, and such a surprise! I can't wait for classes to begin again after the break.

Next term Emma and I will have to work even harder if we're going to pass our grade exams. To tell you the truth I'm a bit nervous. I've never taken a ballet exam before. Angela's bound to breeze through – she's been dancing for so long. I'm going to work extra hard, though, and maybe I'll do as well as her, or even better!

Wish me luck!

Love

Lou

PS Find out how Em and I do in our exams in DANCING SHOES: MAKING THE GRADE. It'll be out soon!